SEW YOUR OWN UNICORN CAKE PILLOW

by the editors of Klutz

KLUTZ®

KLUTZ

® creates activity books and other great stuff for kids ages 3 to 103. We began our corporate life in 1977 in a garage we shared with a Chevrolet Impala. Although we've outgrown that first office, Klutz galactic headquarters is still staffed entirely by real human beings. For those of you who collect mission statements, here's ours:

Create Wonderful Things • Be Good • Have Fun

Faux fur, needle, embroidery floss, and gold fabric manufactured in China. All other components, Taiwan. 85

Distributed in the UK by
Scholastic UK Ltd
Euston House
24 Eversholt Street
London, NW1 1DB
United Kingdom

Distributed in Australia by
Scholastic Australia Ltd
PO Box 579
Gosford, NSW
Australia 2250

Distributed in Canada by
Scholastic Canada Ltd
604 King Street West
Toronto, Ontario
Canada M5V 1E1

Distributed in Hong Kong by
Scholastic Hong Kong Ltd
Suites 2001-2, Top Glory Tower
262 Gloucester Road
Causeway Bay, Hong Kong

ISBN 978-1-338-35522-2
4 1 5 8 5 7 0 8 8 8

Write Us
We would love to hear your comments regarding this or any of our books.

KLUTZ®
557 Broadway
New York, NY 10012
thefolks@klutz.com

Table of Contents

What You Get

PRECUT FAUX FUR

EMBROIDERY
FLOSS IN
2 COLORS

8 POM-POMS
IN 4 COLORS

SEWING NEEDLE

CAKE DISPLAY

PRECUT GOLD FABRIC

STUFFING

18 PRECUT
FELT SHAPES
IN 6 COLORS

Gather these supplies from home:

Scissors • Pencil
Safety pins (optional)

Safety

Always handle needles with care.
Don't rush the stitches.

Needles are sharp.
If you have a thimble, wear it to protect your
fingertips while stitching.

Keep needles away from
small children, pets, and bare feet.

Store your needles when you're finished working.
You can use the needle holder provided or a pin
cushion of your choice.

If a needle breaks, carefully check
the surrounding area and throw out
broken needle pieces.

If a needle breaks the skin, gently
clean the area and apply a bandage.
Get an adult to help you.

This pillow and accessories are
for decoration only. Do not give
them to small children to play with.
Do not sleep with this pillow.

If the project gets dirty, spot-clean only with
a damp rag and warm water. Do not wash the
pillow in a washing machine.

Store loose strands of floss and
other craft supplies away from
pets and babies.

Use supplies included only for projects in this kit.

Using Floss

The embroidery floss in this book has six thin strands twisted together. When you sew this unicorn cake, you'll only need to use two strands at a time. Here's how you separate the strands.

1 Unwind the bundle of embroidery floss. Cut a strand of floss about 14 inches (35.5 cm) long.

2 Hold the floss gently in one hand, about 1 inch (2.5 cm) from the end.

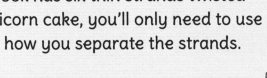

3 With your other hand, pull one strand of floss up . . .

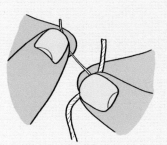

. . . and away from the rest of the bundle.

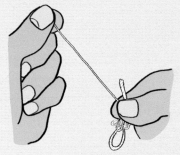

Always separate the threads one at a time.

4 You now have one strand of floss. Repeat Steps 2–3 so you have two strands total.

5 Line up the two strands so the ends meet up. Smooth them down. Now you're ready to sew! Keep extra strands of floss loose and untangled, so you can use them later.

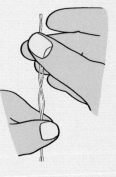

Threading the Needle

1 Tie a knot in one end of your floss. Loop the end across the main part of the strand . . .

. . . then loop the end under and through . . .

. . . and finally pull the end so the knot closes.

2 Moisten the other end of the floss. Pinch the end to help make it pointy.

3 Hold the needle in one hand and push the pointy end of the thread through the loop or eye of the needle.

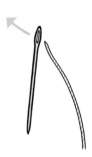

4 Your needle is now threaded! There are two tails of floss. The long end with the knot will sew in and out of the fabric. The short end should hang about 4 inches (10 cm) past the needle to help keep the floss in place.

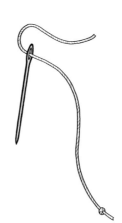

TIP
You can tie a few knots in the same place to make a chunkier knot.

Whip Stitch

How do you whip up a Unicorn Cake Pillow? With a whip stitch! It's how you'll sew pieces of fabric together. Start with the horn before moving on to the rest.

The horn fabric has two straight edges and one curved edge.

What You Need

Gold horn * Stuffing * White floss
Needle * Pencil (optional)

1 Thread a needle with white floss (page 7).

2 Fold the horn so the straight edges meet with the right (shiny) side facing in.

3 Starting from the curved edge, poke the needle through both layers of fabric, and make sure the knot is secure.

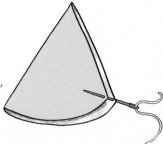

4 Loop the thread around to the back and poke the needle up through both layers of the fabric to make one whip stitch.

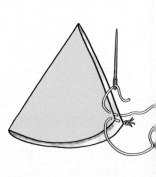

5 Keep stitching all the way around until you reach the pointy tip. Finish your floss (page 12).

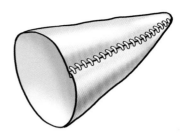

6 Turn the fabric inside out so the shiny side is facing out.

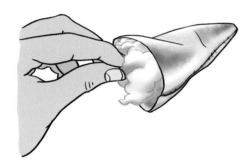

7 Add a little stuffing to the inside, and use your finger or a pencil to push it to the end.

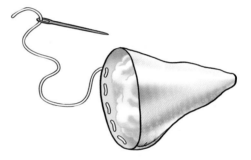

8 Once the horn is full of stuffing, make loose stitches all the way around the open edge of the horn, about ½ inch (13 mm) from the edge.

9 Pull the floss tight so the opening bunches up. This technique is called gathering.

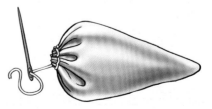

10 Make a few extra stitches through the bottom edge of the horn. Don't finish your floss just yet! Set the horn aside for now.

Best Face Forward

Is your unicorn happy or sleepy? Flip the eyes up or down to choose the right personality.

What You Need

Precut felt eyes x2
Rectangular fur * Black floss
Needle * Scissors

1 Spread out the furry rectangle in front of you with the fur facing up. The long sides will be the top and bottom of the cake.

2 Line up the eyes in the middle of the rectangle. Make them about 1½ inches (4 cm) apart, and about 1½ inches (4 cm) below the top edge.

3 With a needle threaded with black floss, push the needle up through the back of the fabric and the felt.

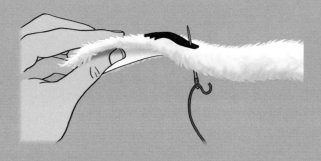

4 Push the needle down through the front of the felt and the fabric, close to where it came up.

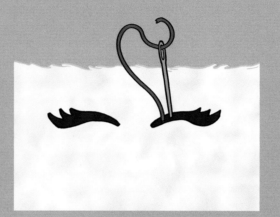

5 Pull firmly on your thread to make one straight stitch on the top of the eye.

6 Keep making little stitches along the eye with your thread. When you're finished, it will look like there's a gap between each stitch.

TIP
If the faux fur sticks in some of your seams, carefully use the pointy end of the needle to pull them out.

Finishing Your Stitches

When you finish stitching or run out of thread, don't let your floss fly away! Make a knot so your stitches stay strong.

1 Turn the fabric over so that you're looking at the wrong side. Poke the needle under one of the nearby stitches (not through the fur) to create a loop.

2 Slide the needle through the loop and pull. This will make a knot close to the fabric.

3 Repeat Steps 1–2 to make an extra strong knot. Then trim the thread close to the fabric.

Make Two Ears

What You Need

Fur ears x2 * Gold ears x2
White floss * Needle
Safety pins (optional)

1 Place one fur ear and one gold ear "right sides together." This means the fur and the shiny side both face each other on the inside. Pin the pieces together, if you'd like.

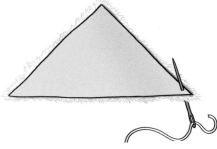

2 Make sure the longest side of the triangle is on the bottom. Start at the bottom corner. With a threaded needle, poke up through both layers of fabric.

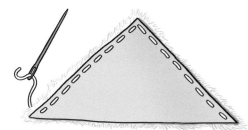

3 Make straight stitches (page 11, Steps 3–5) around both short edges of the ear. Do not sew the long bottom edge.

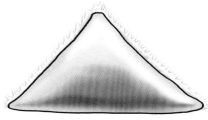

4 Finish your floss (page 12). Then flip the ear inside out.

5 Repeat Steps 1–4 to make the other ear. Set the ears aside for now.

Sew the Side!

What You Need

Cake in progress (page 10)
White floss * Needle * Scissors

1 Line up the short edges of the fur with the right side facing in.

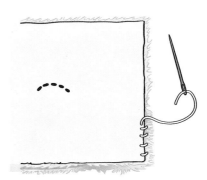

2 Starting at one corner, whip stitch (pages 8–9) along the edge.

Sweet sewing skills!

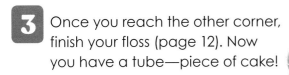

3 Once you reach the other corner, finish your floss (page 12). Now you have a tube—piece of cake!

14

Sew The Bottom

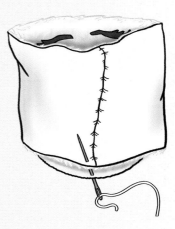

What You Need

White felt circle
Cake in progress * White floss
Needle * Scissors
Safety pins (optional)

1 Making sure the right (furry) sides face in, line up the edge of the **felt circle** with the bottom edge of the tube.

2 The seam you sewed on page 14 is the back of the cake, so start your stitches at the seam. With a needle threaded with white floss, whip stitch the felt circle to the faux fur.

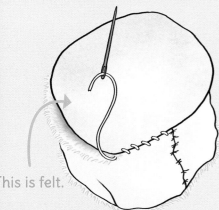

This is felt.

3 Stitch all the way around the edge until you get back to where you started.

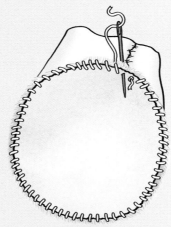

4 Flip the body inside out so the furry side is on the outside.

When you run out of floss, don't worry! Finish your floss (page 12) and start again from that spot with new floss when you're ready.

Add the Ears

What You Need

Finished ears (page 13)
Cake in progress
White floss * Needle * Scissors
Safety pins (optional)

1 Fold the bottom tips of the ear in so they overlap. It's OK if they don't stay folded—you'll sew them in place.

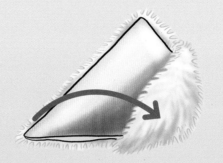

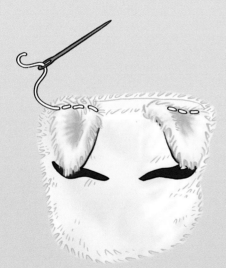

2 Lay the body face up on your work surface and place the ears over the face so the bottoms (unsewn ends) are pointing up, just past the top edge. Make a few stitches to hold them in place.

3 Flip the body inside-out so the furry side is on the inside.

Top It All Off

1 Line up the top edge of the body with the edges of the **fur circle**, making sure the furry side is facing in. The ears will be sandwiched between the top and the body pieces, and the bottom of the ears will stick out from the fabric a bit.

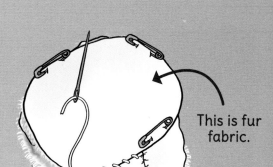

This is fur fabric.

2 Thread a needle with white floss. Sew all along the edges using whip stitch, leaving a 2-inch (5 cm) gap at the back.

Take off any safety pins before you sew over them. Be careful when you sew the ears, so you make sure you are sewing all the layers.

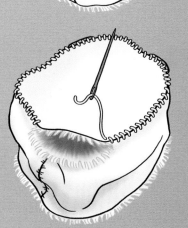

At this point, it looks like the fur is trapped inside—that's OK! You are going to sew the pieces "right sides together." You will leave a gap in the line of stitches, making a hole to pull the furry side through.

3 Turn the unicorn cake inside out through the gap. Voilà! The ears are magically sewn in place!

4 Prep the stuffing by pulling it apart with your fingers, so it's nice and fluffy and even. Add handfuls of stuffing to the hole in the unicorn until the inside is filled up.

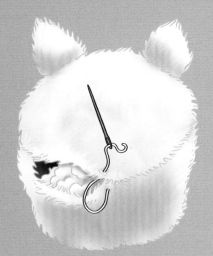

5 Once the unicorn cake is stuffed as much as you like it, close up the hole using ladder stitch (page 19).

Don't give up! Unicorns believe in you!

Ladder Stitch

\/\/\/\/\/\/\/\/\/\/\/\/\/\/\/\/\/\/

- - - - - - - - - - ⚡★⚡ - - - - - - - - - -

Use this magical stitch to close up a gap between two pieces of fabric. Even though you're sewing on the "right" side, the stitches become invisibe!

- - - - - - - - - - ⚡★⚡ - - - - - - - - - -

⭐**1** Start with a threaded needle (page 7). Push your needle up from the inside of the gap so that the knot is inside the fabric.

⭐**2** Make a straight line with your thread across the gap to the opposite fabric.

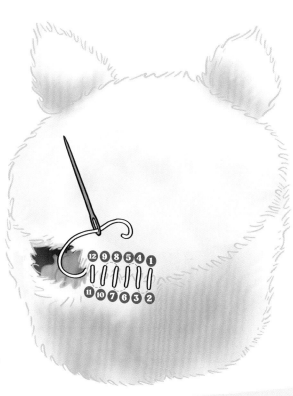

⭐**3** Then pass the needle underneath the fabric and up. . .

⭐**4** . . . and then straight across to the opposite fabric.

⭐**5** Repeat Steps 3–4 (following the numbers) to close the gap. Pull the thread tight. Pull your needle through the finished seam a few times to secure the floss in place.

If your cake is round and puffy, there are a few ways to help shape it:

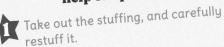

⭐**1** Take out the stuffing, and carefully restuff it.

⭐**2** Smoosh the center of the top down. When it pops up, the top will look flatter.

⭐**3** Tell everyone you made a unicorn marshmallow pillow. Adorable!

Add the Horn

1 Line up the horn so it is centered between the two ears, and a little bit behind them.

2 With a threaded needle, attach the horn to the head with stitches that go all the way around the base of the horn.

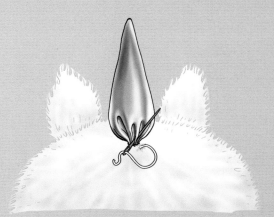

3 Finish your floss (page 12).

The *Uniclassic*

Add pom-poms and flower meringues (muh-RANGS), for this picture-perfect look.

If you like it, put a meringue on it.

1 With a threaded needle, poke the needle up through the back of one petal near the tip.

2 Repeat Step 1 with each petal to the left all the way around.

3 Once you have strung all the petals, poke the needle down through the center of the flower, pull tight, and tie a knot. This will gather all the petals in the meringue shape!

4 Repeat Steps 1–3 to make more meringues with the felt flowers.

5 Attach one meringue by making a stitch in the unicorn's fur, then poking through the base of the meringue.

6 Poke back through the fur, finishing with a knot.

7 Arrange the other meringues, leaves, and pom-poms clustered around the horn and ears, and attach them following Steps 5–6.

Daisy Chain

Combine the pom-poms and the flowers into a fancy floral crown.

1 The petals on a felt flower have a rounded edge and a pointy edge. Using a pair of scissors, snip off the pointy edge of each petal so they are nice and round. Repeat with the other flowers.

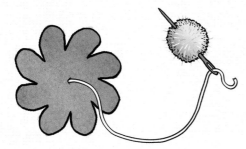

2 With a threaded needle, make one stitch that goes up through the middle of the flower and the pom-pom and back down.

3 Make an ending knot at the back of the flower, but don't snip your floss! Just put the finished daisy aside with the tail hanging off the back.

4 Repeat Steps 1–3 with the other flowers and pom-poms until you've made 8 daisies.

5 Stick the daisies and leaves in a line just below the ears by threading the needle with the tail of a daisy, and poking through the fur along the forehead of the unicorn, making one or two stitches (page 23, Steps 5–6).

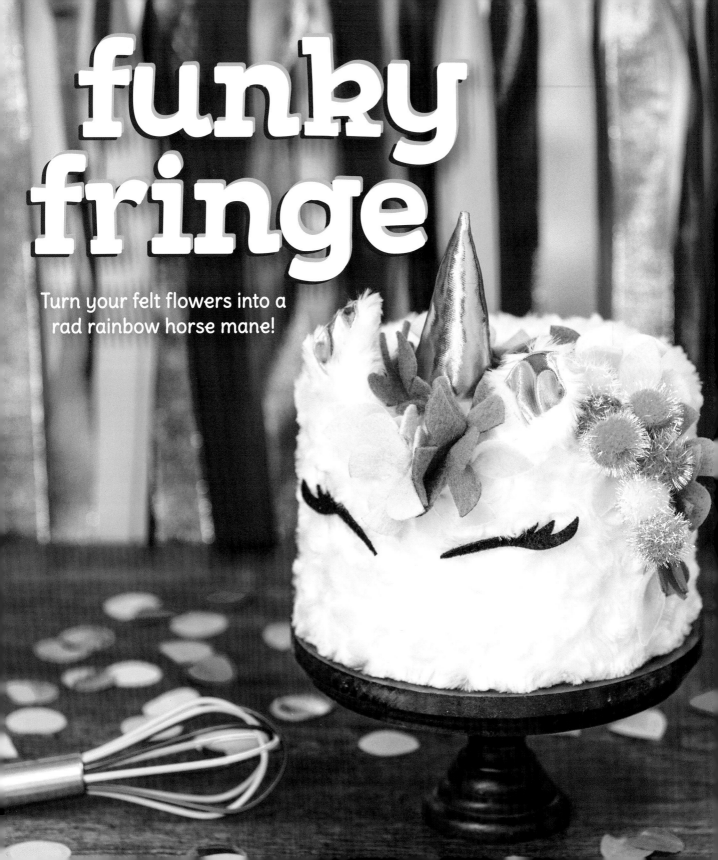

funky fringe

Turn your felt flowers into a rad rainbow horse mane!

1 Cut each purple, pink, and blue flower in half to make 18 pieces.

2 Line up two pieces along their straight edges so they overlap a little, and attach them with a few whip stitches.

3 With the threaded needle, make a few stitches to attach each pair one at a time to the unicorn's forehead. Make sure the knots are strong and secure.

4 Repeat Steps 1–3 with the other pieces, clustering them around the horn and ears.

5 To make a tassel, string three pom-poms together with a threaded needle and attach them to the fur with a few stitches. Finish your floss.

1 Use your scissors to carefully snip around the flower, dividing each petal into three smaller strips. Then cut the entire flower in half to make two pieces. Repeat with the other flowers and leaves.

2 Line up the pieces on either side of the horn and across the top of the head.

3 Stick the pieces onto the unicorn's head with a few whip stitches (page 8).

4 To make the Pegasus wings, whip stitch three pieces on either side of the unicorn body, with the straight edges facing up. Finish your floss (page 12).

Sew together colorful stacks of felt!

Take a peek around your home or local craft store, and check out more ways to decorate!

Make birthday candles out of pipe cleaners and tissue paper.

Glue beads around the edges for some fancy frill.

Add fuzzy friends to wooden skewers and stick the pointy end into the seams.

Yay! Display

What You Need

2 stand pieces ✳ Cake plate
(Gather the pieces from the
cardboard punch out)

Put together the cake stand and give
your unicorn a spot to sparkle!

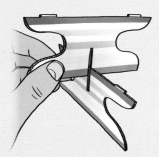

1 Slide the stand together in
an "X" shape.

2 Fold down the scallops on
the cake plate.

3 Place the cake plate on top of
the stand. There are four slots
where the stand will fit into the
cake plate.

credits

Head Baker: Maria Rogers

Designers: Kristin Carder & Vanessa Han

Technical Illustrator: Luke Newell

Photographer: Michael Miranda

Buyer: Roxy Leung

Package Designer: Owen Keating

Editorial Director: Caitlin Harpin

Unicorn Wrangler: Gina Kim

Manager of Product Integrity: Sam Walker

Special thanks to: Stacy Lellos, Netta Rabin, Kim Rogers, Hannah Rogge & Mike Chan

Get creative with more from **KLUTZ**

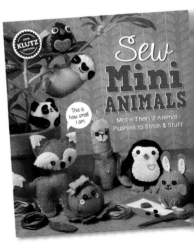

Looking for more goof-proof activities, sneak peeks, and giveaways? Find us online!

 KlutzCertified   KlutzCertified   KlutzCertified   KlutzCertified   Klutz

Klutz.com • thefolks@klutz.com • 1-800-737-4123